THE SAINT NICHOLAS DAY SNOW

BY CHARLOTTE RIGGLE

ILLUSTRATED BY R.J. HUGHES

To Asa, with love -C.R.

To my nephews: may you grow in grace and wisdom -R.J.H.

ISBN: 978-0-9846124-5-1

PHOENIX FLAIR PRESS

COPYRIGHT 2017

charlotteriggle.com

om says I have to pick up all the blocks before Elizabeth comes over. I tell her there are always blocks on the floor at Elizabeth's house, but she says it doesn't matter. I have to pick them up anyway.

I don't mind, though, because Elizabeth is going to stay at our house all day today, and she's going to spend the night tonight. Her parents are going to visit her nana, and she's staying with us.

"Mom!" I shout. "Mom! Is Elizabeth going to help us make St. Nicholas cookies?"

"Yes, of course," Mom says. "We'll make snowball cookies this morning. You and Elizabeth can help."

I hear a car in the driveway. "Elizabeth is here!"

St. Nicholas
Ragnavas Church

Ο ναός του Αγίου
Νικολάου Ραγκαβά

Athens,
Greece

Before 849 a.d.

E lizabeth and her mom come in. My dad goes out to help Elizabeth's dad bring in all her stuff.

"We're going to make snowball cookies!" I tell Elizabeth.

"Can we have a snowball fight?" asks Peter.

"No, silly," Elizabeth says. "You can't have a snowball fight because there isn't any snow."

"But it could snow," says Peter.

"It could," says Elizabeth's dad. "The weather forecast says rain. But I wanted to get an early start, just in case it snows."

Elizabeth's mom and dad give her hugs and kisses before they go. "Tell Nana I love her!" Elizabeth says.

ST. NICHOLAS
CHURCH

WORTH,
ENGLAND

CA. 870

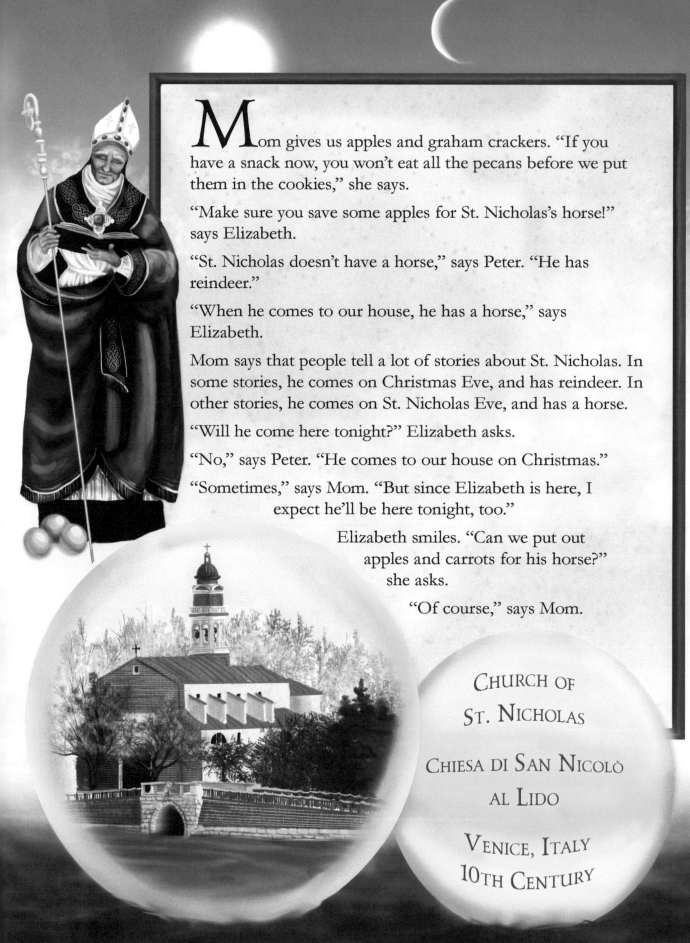

Mom gives us apples and graham crackers. "If you have a snack now, you won't eat all the pecans before we put them in the cookies," she says.

"Make sure you save some apples for St. Nicholas's horse!" says Elizabeth.

"St. Nicholas doesn't have a horse," says Peter. "He has reindeer."

"When he comes to our house, he has a horse," says Elizabeth.

Mom says that people tell a lot of stories about St. Nicholas. In some stories, he comes on Christmas Eve, and has reindeer. In other stories, he comes on St. Nicholas Eve, and has a horse.

"Will he come here tonight?" Elizabeth asks.

"No," says Peter. "He comes to our house on Christmas."

"Sometimes," says Mom. "But since Elizabeth is here, I expect he'll be here tonight, too."

Elizabeth smiles. "Can we put out apples and carrots for his horse?" she asks.

"Of course," says Mom.

CHURCH OF
ST. NICHOLAS

CHIESA DI SAN NICOLÒ
AL LIDO

VENICE, ITALY
10TH CENTURY

Mom gets out all the ingredients for the cookies. I get out the cups and the spoons. Mom runs the mixer while Elizabeth and I take turns measuring the ingredients and dumping them into the bowl.

"What if St. Nicholas can't find me?" Elizabeth asks.

"He'll find you," says Mom.

Pretty soon, the cookie racks are full of cookies fresh from the oven. They smell so good! Mom lets us each eat one while it's warm. "We'll decorate them when they're cool," she says.

"Can I help decorate the cookies?" asks Peter.

"No," says Dad. "You are going to your godparents' house. We can't get everyone to church in our car tomorrow, so you're going to spend the night with them."

"Yay!" says Peter. "That's better than cookies!"

REFORMED CHURCH OF
SAINT NICHOLAS

REFORMIERTE KIRCHE
ST. NIKLAUS

OLTINGEN, SWITZERLAND

11TH CENTURY

When we eat lunch, Elizabeth tells me that she always has candy and treats in her shoes when she gets up on St. Nicholas Day. I tell her that my parents always give Peter and me Christmas books on St. Nicholas Day.

"What does St. Nicholas put in your shoes?" Elizabeth asks.

"He doesn't put anything in our shoes," Peter says. "We get candy and stuff in our stockings, because St. Nicholas put gold in some girl's stockings."

"He did not!" says Elizabeth. "He put gold in their shoes."

"Stockings!" says Peter.

"Shoes!" says Elizabeth.

"Hold on, kids," says Mom.

"It was stockings!" says Peter. Mom gives him her look. He stares back at her, then looks down. "Sorry," he says.

St. Nicholas Church

Nikolaikirche

Leipzig, Germany

1165

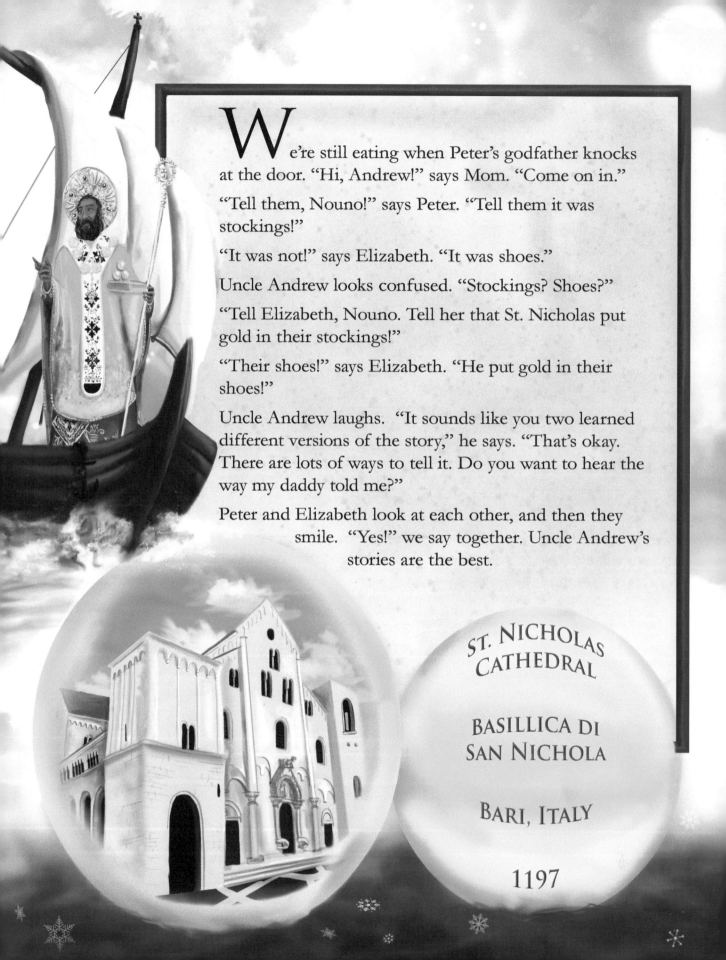

We're still eating when Peter's godfather knocks at the door. "Hi, Andrew!" says Mom. "Come on in."

"Tell them, Nouno!" says Peter. "Tell them it was stockings!"

"It was not!" says Elizabeth. "It was shoes."

Uncle Andrew looks confused. "Stockings? Shoes?"

"Tell Elizabeth, Nouno. Tell her that St. Nicholas put gold in their stockings!"

"Their shoes!" says Elizabeth. "He put gold in their shoes!"

Uncle Andrew laughs. "It sounds like you two learned different versions of the story," he says. "That's okay. There are lots of ways to tell it. Do you want to hear the way my daddy told me?"

Peter and Elizabeth look at each other, and then they smile. "Yes!" we say together. Uncle Andrew's stories are the best.

ST. NICHOLAS
CATHEDRAL

BASILLICA DI
SAN NICHOLA

BARI, ITALY

1197

Uncle Andrew sits down at the table. "You all know the first part," he says. "When St. Nicholas was young, he had a poor neighbor who had three daughters. And the neighbor's oldest daughter was going to sell herself as a slave, so there would be money for her sisters to get married. Right?"

"Right," says Peter. Elizabeth and I nod.

"St. Nicholas didn't want that to happen. So he slipped to their house in the middle of the night, and he tossed a bag of gold in through the window. And the gold landed right in the oldest girl's shoe, but it made such a loud noise that it woke up the girls and their father and the dog, and St. Nicholas barely got away!"

"See! It was shoes!" says Elizabeth.

"Later on," says Uncle Andrew, "St. Nicholas decided to go back with more gold, so the second daughter could marry, too. This time, he decided to be very, very quiet.

"What did he do?" I ask.

ST. NICHOLAS CHURCH

SINT-NIKLAASKERK

GHENT, BELGIUM

CA. 13TH CENTURY

"H e peeked in, and he saw that the girls had hung their stockings by the window. So he reached in through the window, and he slipped the gold into one of the stockings."

"Stockings!" says Peter to Elizabeth.

"And the third time, of course, the father caught St. Nicholas outside his house, so that gold didn't go in a shoe or a stocking. St. Nicholas just handed it to the man, and asked him not to tell anyone."

"But he told," I say.

"Yes, he told his daughters, and his daughters told their friends. And one said that St. Nicholas put gold in her shoe, and the other said that he put gold in her stocking."

NÚPSSTAÐUR
CHURCH OF ST.
NICHOLAS

NÚPSSTAÐAKIRKJA
ST. NICHOLAS

NÚPSSTAÐUR,
ICELAND

CA. 1200

"So you're both right," says Uncle Andrew, standing up. "And you, Peter, need to go get your overnight bag." He looks at Mom. "It started snowing when I was coming over, and I want to get home before the sidewalks are too buried."

"It's snowing?" Peter says.

We all jump up from the table and run to the door.

"It's snowing!" I say.

Dad comes to the door and looks at the sky. "I think I'll get my coat and go run my errands now," Dad says. "Just in case it keeps snowing."

EIDSBORG STAVE CHURCH OF ST. NICHOLAS

EIDSBORG STAVKYRKJE AV NICOLAUS (NIKULS) AV BARI

TOKKE, NORWAY

CA. 1250

After Peter and Uncle Andrew and Dad leave, Elizabeth and I go outside and catch snowflakes on our mittens. The flakes are getting bigger.

"Can St. Nicholas ride his horse in the snow?" I ask Elizabeth.

"I don't know," she says. "But if he can't, maybe he'll bring his reindeer."

I think about that one. "We'll have to leave extra carrots," I say. "Just in case it keeps snowing."

Elizabeth starts shivering, so we go inside. Mom makes hot chocolate for us.

MAR NICOLA

كنيسة مار نقولا

BEIT JALA, PALESTINE

CA. 1300

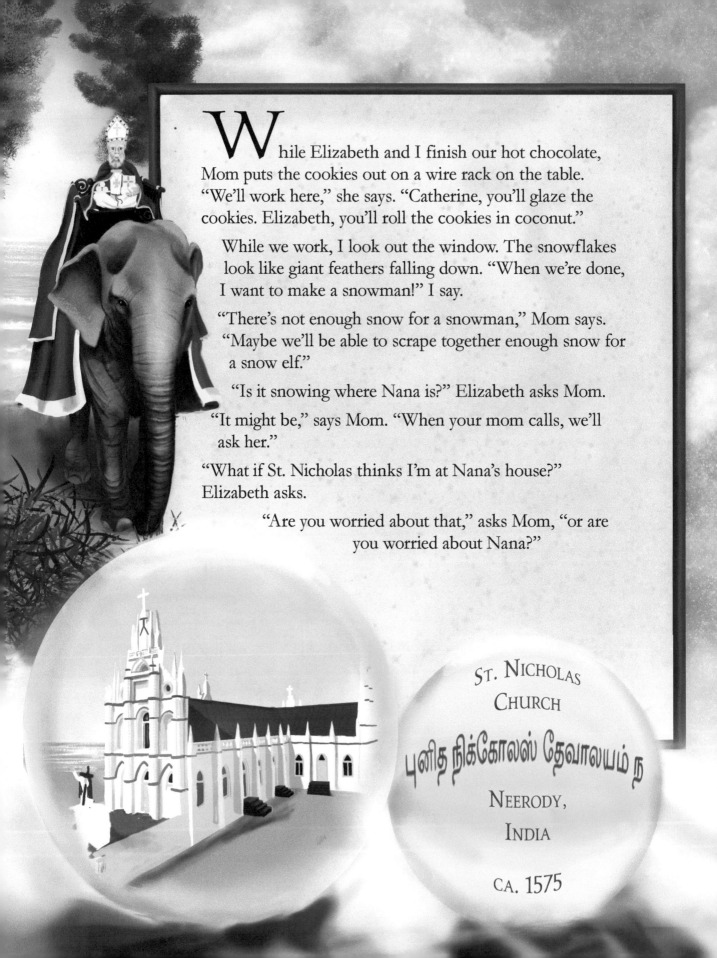

While Elizabeth and I finish our hot chocolate, Mom puts the cookies out on a wire rack on the table. "We'll work here," she says. "Catherine, you'll glaze the cookies. Elizabeth, you'll roll the cookies in coconut."

While we work, I look out the window. The snowflakes look like giant feathers falling down. "When we're done, I want to make a snowman!" I say.

"There's not enough snow for a snowman," Mom says. "Maybe we'll be able to scrape together enough snow for a snow elf."

"Is it snowing where Nana is?" Elizabeth asks Mom.

"It might be," says Mom. "When your mom calls, we'll ask her."

"What if St. Nicholas thinks I'm at Nana's house?" Elizabeth asks.

"Are you worried about that," asks Mom, "or are you worried about Nana?"

St. Nicholas Church

புனித நிக்கோலஸ் தேவாலயம் ந

Neerody,
India

CA. 1575

E lizabeth is quiet for a moment. Then she says, "Both."

"Would you like to pray for your nana?" Mom asks.

Elizabeth nods.

We go to the icon corner, and Mom lights the candles and the incense. Then we make the cross, and say the Lord's Prayer, and then Mom says the prayer for the sick.

At the end of the prayer, Mom says, "Through the prayers of our holy fathers, especially St. Nicholas the Wonderworker of Myra," and we all say "Amen."

Elizabeth blows out the candles.

ST. NICHOLAS
CHURCH

IGLESIA DE SAN NICOLAS

SAN CRISTOBAL,
CHIAPAS, MEXICO

CA. 1621

When Dad comes in, he stamps snow off his shoes and shakes snow off his hat. "This seems to be turning into a regular snowstorm," he says.

"Mom," I say. "Mom, when should we put our shoes out for St. Nicholas?"

"When do you put your shoes out?" Mom asks Elizabeth.

"We always do it right before bedtime," she says.

"Well, then," Mom says, "that's what we'll do."

"But what if he doesn't come?" asks Elizabeth.

"He'll come," Mom says.

ST. NICHOLAS
NAVAL CATHEDRAL
Никольский морской
собор
ST. PETERSBURG, RUSSIA

1760

After evening prayers, Elizabeth and I sit down by the kitchen door and take off our shoes. Mom hands us each an apple and a carrot. We put a carrot in one shoe and an apple in the other one. Dad opens the kitchen door. Big, fat snowflakes are still falling outside. The grass and the swings are all covered in snow.

"I think we need more carrots," I tell Mom.

"Why?" she asks.

"Because St. Nicholas might have to bring his reindeer," Elizabeth says.

Dad looks at the snow. "You have a point," he says. He gives us more carrots.

We put the shoes outside in the snow.

BASILICA OF
SAINT NICHOLAS

BASILIEK VAN DE
HEILIGE NICOLAAS

AMSTERDAM,
NETHERLANDS
1887

W hile Mom helps Elizabeth in the bathroom, I get my flashlight and my Christmas books and hide them under the blankets.

After we get in bed, Mom kisses each of us on top of the head. "Good night, girls," she says, turning off the light. "Enjoy the books."

"Good night, Mom," I say.

"Does she always know you're going to read after bedtime?" Elizabeth asks.

"I think she knows everything," I say. And Elizabeth and I read Christmas stories until we fall asleep.

SEOUL ANGLICAN CATHEDRAL
CHURCH OF STS. MARY
AND NICHOLAS
서울 성공회 성당 성도 메리와 니콜라스
SEOUL, SOUTH KOREA
1891

ST. NICHOLAS RUSSIAN
ORTHODOX CATHEDRAL

WOOLLOONGABBA,
QUEENSLAND,
AUSTRALIA
1930

"Wake up, girls!" says Mom. I rub my eyes. Elizabeth pushes herself up. "Would you like pancakes and cookies for breakfast?"

"Breakfast?" I say. "We can't have breakfast. We're going to church!"

"We can't go to church this morning," Mom says. "There's too much snow."

I look out the window. The snow must be a hundred feet deep!

"Can we make a snowman?" I ask.

"What about Nana?" Elizabeth asks.

ST. NICHOLAS CATHEDRAL

WASHINGTON D.C.,
USA

1930

M om sits down on the bed. "I just talked to your mom, Elizabeth. Your nana is fine. Your parents are going to stay another night with your nana because of the snow. That means you get to spend one more night with us."

Elizabeth stares at Mom. "She's really okay?"

"Yes," says Mom. "She's really okay."

Elizabeth takes a deep breath, and then she throws her arms around Mom. "She's okay! Nana's okay!"

"Can we make a snowman?" I ask again.

"Let's have cookies first!" Elizabeth says.

ORTHODOX CATHEDRAL OF
ST. NICHOLAS OF MYRA

CATEDRAL ORTODOXA
DE SAN NICOLÁS DE MIRA

HAVANA, CUBA

2004

W hen we get downstairs, Dad is making pancakes.

"Happy St. Nicholas Day!" I say.

"Happy St. Nicholas Day!" says Dad.

Elizabeth opens the kitchen door and pulls the shoes inside. "Look Catherine!" she says. The shoes are full of oranges and chocolate coins and candy canes. And snow.

"And look!" I say, There's a book for you, too! There's even one for Peter!"

"We'll say prayers after breakfast," Mom says. "And then we can go outside and make a snowman."

"Can we make a snow bishop, and a snow horse?" I ask.

"I don't know how to make a snow horse," Mom says, "But we can try!

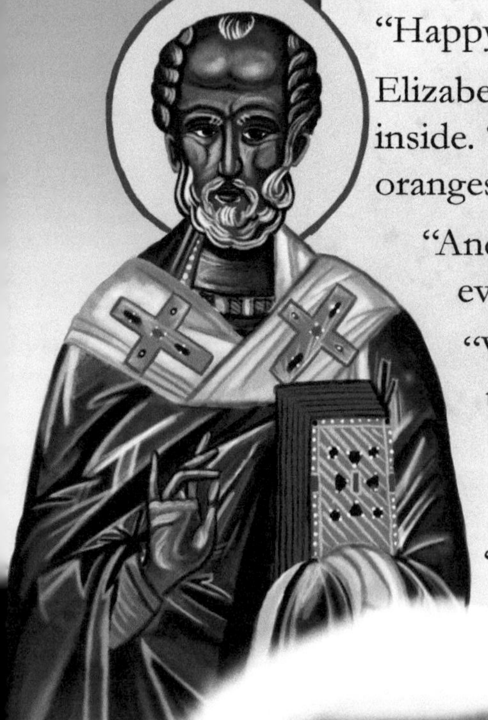

ST. NICHOLAS
GREEK ORTHODOX
CHURCH
&
NATIONAL SHRINE

NEW YORK CITY,
NEW YORK, USA

1916; 2018

THE ANCIENT CHURCH
WHERE St. NICHOLAS
WORKED & WAS BURIED
(NOW RUINED)

ANCIENT MYRA, LYCIA
MODERN DEMRE, TURKEY

CA. FIRST CENTURY

WHO WAS ST. NICHOLAS?

St. Nicholas wasn't an elf, of course. And he didn't live at the North Pole. He was a man, born in the year 270 (or perhaps 280) in the Greek village of Patara in what is now Turkey. By most accounts, he was the beloved only child of his parents. They died while he was still young, and he inherited their fortune. But rather than choosing a life of luxury, he chose to live humbly and to serve the poor. Before long, he was made Bishop of Myra, the capital city of the province of Lycia.

In 303, Roman emperor Diocletian began his fierce persecution of Christians. Bishop Nicholas, along with other leaders of the Church, was arrested and imprisoned. Somewhere along the way, he took a blow to the face that smashed the bone between his eyes. When that healed, his broad nose was decidedly crooked.

Bishop Nicholas was released from prison when Emperor Constantine ended the persecutions. He returned to Myra, where he served until his death on December 6, 343 (or perhaps 352). He was buried in the cathedral where he had served.

That's just about all that we know with certainty about him. It's not that anything about him has been forgotten. It's that, because people loved him so dearly and so well, they talked about him. They told stories, lots of stories. They told what they knew, and what they remembered, and what other people had told them. And sometimes one story would get mixed up with another story, or part of it would get forgotten. The rough edges of real life got smoothed out here and there to make the stories easier to remember. Because that's what happens when people tell stories for nearly two thousand years.

You can read many stories of St. Nicholas at charlotteriggle.com/saint-nicholas-day-snow.

WHY IS ST. NICHOLAS CELEBRATED ON DECEMBER 6?

From the earliest years of the Church, Christians honored saints on the anniversary of their death, not on the anniversary of their birth. And St. Nicholas died on December 6. So, for nearly two thousand years, Christians have honored him every year on December 6.

Some also celebrate St. Nicholas on May 9, commemorating the day, in 1087, St. Nicholas's relics arrived in Bari, Italy. This day is called "The Translation of the Relics of Saint Nicholas from Myra to Bari." Of these two festivals, December 6 is more well known.

NIKOLSKOE/NIKOLSKOYE; 1799, 2012
BERING ISLAND, KAMCHATKA KRAI, RUSSIA

ST. NICHOLAS ORTHODOX CHURCH; CA 1830
ATKA ISLAND, ALASKA, USA

WHY IS ST. NICHOLAS CALLED A SAINT?

In English, we use the word *saint* for people, and we use the word *holy* for God, or for things that are set apart by or for God. We have two words because we took the word *holy* from the Greek word *hagios,* and *saint* from the Latin word *sanctus.* But the two words really mean the same thing.

In the early Church, the word saint (or holy one) just meant a Christian. You see the word used this way throughout the New Testament. For example, the Apostle Paul addresses his letter to the Ephesians "to the saints who are in Ephesus, and are faithful in Christ Jesus." He was saying that all the Christians in Ephesus were God's holy people.

It's still entirely proper to use the word saint that way. But over time, *saint* came to be used especially for the martyrs, and also for the confessors, the people who had been tortured or imprisoned because they were Christians. It's not that other Christians weren't holy. But, in humility, most Christians chose to honor the martyrs and confessors for the love they had for Christ and for the sacrifice they made.

The confessors were honored with the martyrs because, in so many cases, anyone who was one could just as easily have been the other. The blow that smashed St. Nicholas's face could have killed him; if it had, he'd have been a martyr instead of a confessor.

When a new generation of Christians faced persecution and martyrdom, the lives of the saints gave them courage and hope. The stories reminded them that their trials had already been faced by others. With the help of God and the saints, they could face them, too.

After the emperor Constantine issued the Edict of Toleration, martyrdom became less common. And over time, *saint,* or *holy one,* came to be used for more people. The prophets and apostles were called saints. So were monks and nuns who gave up wealth and power to live in constant prayer and fasting. And later, still others were called saints because of the way their lives showed the love of God. It's not that they were perfect. But they were holy. They were saints.

And so we call the fourth century Bishop of Myra Saint Nicholas.

DO ORTHODOX CHRISTIANS PRAY TO SAINTS?

The most beloved hymn of the Orthodox Church says, "Christ is risen from the dead, trampling down death by death, and upon those in the tomb bestowing life." Orthodox Christians believe that, in his Resurrection, Christ destroyed the power of death. Death can't separate us from God, or from each other. We are alive in Christ.

Orthodox Christians also believe in asking each other for prayers and for help in times of need. We can each ask God for ourselves, of course. And we do. But in love and humility, we also turn to each other.

"Each other" includes our family and friends. And it includes the people we call saints. The saints are no longer distracted by earthly cares and physical needs. They can truly pray without ceasing. And so we ask them to help us and pray for us.

ST. NICHOLAS CHAPEL AND SCHOOL

TEMA, GHANA; 2006

Why Is St. Nicholas Sometimes Called Santa Claus?

St. Nicholas was always a popular saint. By the Middle Ages, there were thousands of churches dedicated to him, with more than four hundred in England alone. Then came Henry VIII and Edward VI. Under their rule, shrines were destroyed, statues were smashed, and religious art was painted over. Anything that seemed too Catholic was ruthlessly suppressed. Even the celebration of Christmas. Especially the veneration of saints.

Most early English settlers did not bring saints to America. But the Dutch settlers did. The Dutch call Nicholas *Sinterklaas*, a shortened form of *Sint Nicolaas*. Because of this, many Americans were reintroduced to St. Nicholas through their Dutch-descended neighbors, and called him *Santa Claus*.

Why Does Santa Claus Come on Christmas Eve?

In the 1800s, and particularly in the latter part of that century, America was a divided country. Urban and rural, immigrants and native born, wealthy and poor seemed to live different lives. They didn't understand each other. They didn't even much like each other. And so it happened that, during this time, specifically American customs began to develop, to help unify the fragmented nation.

Many of the Christmas customs we know today were created during this time. The festivities were designed to feel old-fashioned and sentimental. People decorated their homes with evergreen and holly. Americans learned of the German tradition of Christmas trees, and soon adopted it wholesale. People began sending Christmas cards. Soon, businesses closed to give employees Christmas Day off so they could celebrate with friends and family.

And, thanks to an 1823 poem by Clement Clark Moore, children began hanging stockings on Christmas Eve for St. Nicholas to fill. The title of the poem is "A Visit from St. Nicholas," but nearly everyone knows it as "The Night Before Christmas."

Moore was a scholar, and he surely knew that St. Nicholas's feast day was December 6. But in the 1800s, most people in America didn't keep saint days. St. Nicholas had always had something of an association with Christmas, because his feast day falls during Advent, during the time of preparation for Christmas. So Moore used his artistic license to move St. Nicholas's visit to Christmas Eve.

ÉGLISE SAINT NICOLAS; 1961
ST-NICOLAS (LÉVIS), QUEBEC, CANADA

ST NICHOLAS CATHOLIC CHURCH; 1857
SANTA CLAUS, INDIANA, USA

IF ST. NICHOLAS DOESN'T BRING GIFTS TO CHILDREN, WHO DOES?

Catherine, Elizabeth, and Peter argued about whether St. Nicholas brings gifts on December 6 or Christmas Eve. They didn't know that, in other countries, there are other gift-givers. And the other gift-givers often bring gifts on other days.

RELIGIOUS GIFT-GIVERS

In Germany, Martin Luther decided that the Christ Child would bring gifts to the children on Christmas Eve. That custom spread from Germany throughout the world. The Christ Child is the most common gift-giver throughout large parts of Europe and Latin America.

In some parts of Italy, St. Lucia brings gifts on her feast day, December 13. She arrives on a donkey with an assistant named Castaldo. In other parts of Italy, children receive gifts from La Befana, an old woman who followed the Magi to look for the baby Jesus. On January 5, Epiphany Eve, she gives gifts to all children for the sake of the Babe she couldn't find.

St. Basil brings gifts to children in Greece and Cyprus on his feast day, January 1. In some Spanish-speaking countries and parts of Central Europe, the three wise men who brought gold, frankincense, and myrrh to the infant Jesus bring gifts to children on Epiphany, January 6.

SECULAR GIFT-GIVERS

Various old men, called Father Christmas, Father Frost, Old Man Christmas, or Papa Noel are the most common secular gift-givers. They personify Christmas or winter. In Iceland, the Yule Lads are the gift-givers. They bring small gifts each night on the final thirteen nights of Advent.

In Scandinavia, Christmas gifts are frequently brought by the short, jolly, white-bearded Christmas Gnome. Santa Claus looks a bit like the Christmas Gnome because of Haddon Sundblom. Sundblom is the man who designed the Coca-Cola Santa. Though American-born, his parents were Scandinavian, and he grew up with the tradition of the Christmas Gnome. He incorporated the look of the Gnome into his Santa Claus.

WHERE CAN I LEARN MORE ABOUT ST. NICHOLAS?

You'll find a lot about St. Nicholas at charlotteriggle.com/saint-nicholas-day-snow. But if you want a comprehensive source of information about St. Nicholas online, you really must check out the website of **The St. Nicholas Center,** stnicholascenter.org.

If you prefer books to websites, start with *The Saint Who Would be Santa Claus: the True Life and Trials of Nicholas of Myra* by Adam C. English, published 2012 by Baylor University Press. Then go to the Resources page at charlotteriggle.com/saint-nicholas-day-snow for a longer bibliography.

DOMKIRKE SANKT NIKOLAI — GARÐAR, GREENLAND; 1126

WHAT ARE THE CHURCHES IN *THE SAINT NICHOLAS DAY SNOW*?

St. Nicholas is the most widely revered Christian saint after the Virgin Mary. He's even honored by people who aren't Christians! R.J. Hughes, the illustrator of *The Saint Nicholas Day Snow*, decided to include an image of St. Nicholas and a picture of a church dedicated to St. Nicholas on every spread in the book.

The churches are generally arranged chronologically from the oldest churches in the beginning of the story to the newest at the end. Each image of St Nicholas reflects one way the country featured on the page sees St. Nicholas. Occasionally, they are from the featured church; sometimes they are from a different source in the same era. In some cases, time, war, and cultural changes destroyed older images, and a newer image has been featured.

You can learn more about the churches, images, and artwork at: charlotteriggle.com/saint-nicholas-day-snow.

SPECIAL THANKS

Books take time, passion (a touch of insanity), and a lot of support. Thank you to Jennifer Harshman, Fr. Marty Watt, Vasily Konovalov, the Koinonia for Exceptional Orthodox Families, and our focus group of beta readers, who helped us with editing, image feedback, Elizabeth's abilities (not disabilities), translations, and other details.

Thank you to the St. Nicholas Center for the information, photos, and especially the gallery of churches. This book would have taken much longer without your graciously shared work and resources.

Thank you to all the iconographers whose work brings joy to worship. In particular, to iconographers Luke Dingman, Dimitry Shkolnik, and Randi Sider-Rose, whose work and expertise has graced both this book and its predecessor.

And once again, thank you to Alex Riggle, Justin Hughes, and our families, who supported us when we once again lost our minds and attacked a new vision, even through the insantiy of job and residence changes, and all the extra stress it caused. We couldn't do it without you.

To everyone who has helped us along this journey, thank you!

BASILIQUE SAINT-NICOLAS; CA. 1120 — SAINT-NICOLAS-DE-PORT, FRANCE

KOSTEL SV. MIKULÁŠE; CA. 1400 — CHODUNY-LOUNKY, CZECH REPUBLIC

CATHERINE AND ELIZABETH'S SNOWBALL COOKIES

Many Christians keep the weeks before Christmas as Advent. It's a time of spiritual preparation for Christmas, with fasting, prayer, and almsgiving. The Christmas celebrations start on Christmas day, not before.

But St. Nicholas Day falls during the Advent season. And St. Nicholas Day is a day for celebration. This cookie recipe uses no eggs or dairy, so it meets the requirement of the Advent fast as it's kept by Orthodox Christians.

If you're not keeping the fast, feel free to substitute butter for the coconut oil, and dairy milk for the coconut milk.

COOKIE INGREDIENTS

2 cups flour

2 cups finely chopped pecans

¼ cup sugar

1 cup coconut oil, or 2 sticks of vegan margarine, softened (*Do not use a low-fat margarine or butter substitute!*)

1 tsp vanilla

GLAZE INGREDIENTS

2 1/4 cups confectioners' sugar, sifted

2 Tbsp light corn syrup

2 Tbsp coconut milk, plus a bit more if needed

Snowflake-shaped sprinkles, finely shredded coconut, or bright white sparkling sugar, for decorating

INSTRUCTIONS

1.) Heat the oven to 325°F (163°C). Line cookie sheets with parchment paper.

2.) In a large mixer bowl, combine all cookie ingredients. Beat at low speed until well mixed, scraping the sides of the bowl as often as you need to.

3.) Use your hands to shape rounded teaspoonfuls of the dough into one-inch balls. Put the balls an inch apart on the cookie sheet. Bake 20 to 25 minutes, until they're just barely browned. Cool completely on a rack. (Put waxed paper or a cookie sheet under the rack to reduce the mess when you glaze the cookies!)

4.) Once the cookies are completely cool, use a fork to mix the glaze ingredients in a small bowl until the glaze is completely smooth. You want the glaze to be thin enough to spread over the cookies when you spoon it on. If it's too thick, add more coconut milk, one teaspoon at a time.

5.) Spoon the glaze over the cookies. Before it's completely dry, sprinkle with snowflake-shaped sprinkles, bright white sparkling sugar, or finely shredded coconut.

CHURCH OF ST NICHOLAS AND ST. PANTELEIMON

Боянска църква

SOFIA, BULGARIA, CA. 1000

CPSIA information can be obtained
at www.ICGtesting.com
Printed in the USA
LVHW070047281118
598392LV00005B/103/P